MAD MYTHS:
A TOUCH OF
WIND!

Steve Barlow and
Steve Skidmore

Galaxy

CHIVERS PRESS
BATH

First published 1998
by
Puffin
This Large Print edition published by
Chivers Press
by arrangement with
Penguin Children's Books
2000

ISBN 0 7540 6116 7

British Library Cataloguing in Publication Data available

Barlow, Steve
    A touch of wind.—Large print ed.—(Mad myths)
    1. Odysseus (Greek mythology)—Juvenile fiction
    2. Sirens (Mythology)—Juvenile fiction
    3. Childrens stories 4. Large type books
    I. Title II. Skidmore, Steve
    823. 9'14[J]

ISBN 0-7540-6116-7

Printed and bound in Great Britain by
REDWOOD BOOKS, Trowbridge, Wiltshire

Contents

CHAPTER ONE

OUTWARD BOUND

'I mean, map reading is bad enough . . .'

Andy wasn't listening to Perce. He was desperately trying to hold a large paper map open long enough to read it, while the wind tried just as hard to snatch it out of his fingers.

'. . . and running is worse . . .'

Perce was doing nothing to help. She stood with her arms folded, huddled against the 'bracing' sea breeze that was blowing right through her

1

tracksuit, piercing her skin and whistling round her bones.

'. . . so, put them together, and what have you got?'

'Why don't you tell me?' Andy had finally got the map open and discovered he was holding it upside-down.

'Torture! And they call this an Outward Bound course! I know what I'd call it. What was that thing they had in Spain? Inky-something.'

Eddie Johnson, lying face-down on the shingle, fighting for breath (and losing), raised a purple face and gasped, 'Inquisition.'

'Right! If they'd had our instructors in charge of the Spanish Inky-sition, they wouldn't have needed the rack and thumbscrews, they'd just have sent all their victims out orienteering.' Perce gave the landscape a disgusted look. 'In Bogmouth-on-Sylt,' she added.

Eddie started to say that the Inquisition, being Spanish, would probably have sent prisoners to the Costa Brava, but decided to be sick instead.

2

Perce glowered at the sea. It was still rough from last night's storm, which had kept her awake, rattling the windows of the hostel. This morning, they'd all been kicked out in their tracksuits at a time when even milkmen were still snuggled under their duvets. They'd each been given a map and a compass and told to find their way round the marked course.

So far, the route had led them to a rubbish tip, round the back of the fish-gutting factory, across the Crazy Golf course and now down to the beach. If you could call a mile of pebbles punctuated by breakwaters a beach.

Angry clouds streamed across a sky the colour of a bruise.

'Well, it could be worse,' ventured Andy philosophically.

'How?'

'It could be raining.'

A thin drizzle started. Immediately, it was whipped by the wind into a stinging shower.

'Perfect. Well done, Andy.' Perce tried to pull her head back into her

3

tracksuit like a tortoise. It didn't work.

Andy sighed and shook his compass. The needle fell off.

Well'ard Wally slithered down the dune behind them.

' 'Ullo,' he said. 'Where do we go next?'

'You're supposed to work it out for yourself,' snapped Perce.

'So're you.'

Perce shrugged. She couldn't be bothered to argue, especially as Well'ard was right; of course, that wouldn't have stopped her if she hadn't been cold and wet as well.

Andy gazed along the beach. In the distance, Bogmouth lurked miserably in the mist.

He turned his back on the sodden town and pointed. 'That way.'

Eddie staggered to his feet. 'No more running,' he panted. 'I'll have a heart attack.'

Well'ard sneered. 'Wimp. Dunno why you came on an Outward Bound course. They'd never have you in the SAS.'

Perce and Andy groaned and set off

down the beach. Well'ard's lifelong ambition was to get into the SAS, as he reminded everybody at least a dozen times a day.

As they jogged over the sliding pebbles, Well'ard raced ahead and Eddie trailed behind, complaining bitterly: 'I came for the canoeing and the windsurfing, nobody told me about the running, I wouldn't've come if they'd said they were going to make us do twenty-mile runs every day . . .'

Perce was jogging to a rhythm in her mind that went, I *hate* Bog *mouth*, I *hate* Bog *mouth* . . .

'Where are we going?' she asked Andy.

'Pillbox over there,' Andy panted. 'You know, one of those concrete things they built in the war. That's the next check-point.'

'Does Well'ard know that?'

But Well'ard had run out of puff after his sprint. He'd stopped up ahead and was throwing stones at seagulls.

There was a wail behind them from Eddie. 'I need a rest!'

'In a minute!' Perce peered ahead to

5

find a landmark. 'When we get to that pile of old rags up there.'

'I'll never make it! I've got very small lungs for my height.'

Perce ignored Eddie. She pounded on. Why on earth had she come on this Outward Bound course? Well, to get out of school, obviously, but it had been a terrible mistake. Even school was better than Bogmouth-on-Sylt. It was full of old fogies and everything cost a fortune and the funfair was closed because it was the end of the season and it had hardly stopped raining since they got here . . . I *hate* Bog *mouth*, I *hate* Bog *mouth* . . .

They were quite near the pile of rags now. From a distance, it had just looked like any other pile of rubbish cast up by the storm; but as they got closer, they could see it had a definite shape, almost a human shape . . .

Perce skidded to a halt. Andy stopped and gazed back at her.

'What's up?' He followed her gaze and looked at the pile of rags. 'Oh.'

The bundle wasn't of rags, but of clothes—a cloak of some sort. A bare foot was sticking out from under the pile.

Perce's voice shook. 'He must be a sailor!'

Andy nodded. 'Washed overboard in the storm.'

'Or shipwrecked.'

Well'ard joined them. 'Wossup?' He saw the foot. 'Ooer. Dead, is he?'

Perce swallowed. 'I don't know.'

'Better look, then,' said Well'ard, not moving.

Eddie staggered to a stop beside them, his chest heaving. 'I'm knackered.' He sat down at their feet and slumped against the hunched shape.

'Eddie! Noooo!'

The bundle moved. Eddie gave a strangled scream and shot to his feet. The 'pile of rags' writhed, making coughing sounds. Perce, Andy and Well'ard shrank back.

A man's head, with hair and beard plastered to its face, emerged from the pile and stared about in confusion. A voice croaked, 'What place is this?'

Perce stammered, 'B-B-B-Bogmouth.'

7

The man sighed. 'Never heard of it. It's nowhere near Athens, I suppose?'

Perce stared hard at him. She was sure she'd never seen him before, but there was something about him, almost familiar . . .

'Who are you?' she demanded abruptly.

The stranger raised his eyes to meet hers. 'Odysseus of Ithaca, at your service.'

Eddie and Well'ard stared. Perce gave a resigned nod.

Andy slapped his forehead with the palm of his hand.

'Oh, no!' he howled. 'Not again!'

CHAPTER TWO

A BIG BAG OF WIND

Andy stood with a glazed look on his face. 'It can't be happening again, can it?'

Perce shrugged her shoulders. 'If you mean, "Are we really standing here with yet another mythological nutter?", then yeah, it looks like it.'

Andy shook his head. 'Why is it that any legendary creepo with nothing better to do suddenly gets a burning desire to drop by and do something incredibly nasty to us?'

Andy's concern was understandable. He and Perce had already suffered from the attentions of Ms Dusa, the supply teacher from hell, and Mr O'Taur, a bully of a caretaker in every sense of the word.

Perce tried to look on the bright side. 'But Odysseus wasn't a monster. He was a Greek hero.'

'So what's a Greek hero doing washed up on a beach in Bogmouth-on-Sylt?' asked Eddie.

'Good question,' mused Perce. 'Perhaps we'd better find out.'

'He's not Odysseus, he's just a nutter,' jeered Well'ard. 'A real Greek hero would have a massive sword and—'

He broke off as the man staggered to his feet and produced a massive sword from under his cloak.

'Hmm. So maybe he is a real Greek hero,' Well'ard conceded.

There was an uneasy silence as the four orienteers and the bedraggled figure of Odysseus stared at each other.

Beep beep beep beep beeeeeep! The

silence was shattered by the piercing noise of the alarm on Eddie's watch. Odysseus jumped back in surprise, and swept up his sword to protect himself.

'That sound: it comes from your wrist! Are you gods?'

Perce shook her head. 'Er, no, not that I know of.'

'Strange enchanters?'

'Not enchanters either, although those three *are* strange,' replied Perce, indicating the others.

'Then, in the name of Zeus, who are you?'

'I'm Perce.'

'Her real name's Priscilla,' piped up Eddie. 'It's just that she doesn't like . . .' Eddie tailed off as Perce put her clenched fist against his nose. 'She's Perce,' he said quickly.

Perce pointed. 'The one with the big mouth and nearly flattened nose is Eddie Johnson, that's Andy and the thing over there is Well'ard Wally. He calls himself that because he thinks he's hard.'

'I *am* hard,' growled Well'ard.

'In your dreams,' replied Andy,

inching out of Well'ard's reach, just in case Well'ard decided to demonstrate how hard he was.

'Greetings to you all.' Lowering his sword, Odysseus gazed around. 'I have visited many strange lands in my wanderings, but none as desolate as this. What is the name of this place again?'

'Bogmouth-on-Sylt,' said Eddie, apologetically.

'So, you've been travelling a lot, have you?' enquired Perce.

'Far and wide since I left Troy.'

'Troy who?' asked Andy.

'He means Troy the city, not Troy a person, diphead,' sneered Well'ard. 'The Greek army was attacking it for years and years but they couldn't get in.'

He pointed at Odysseus. 'It was his idea to make a massive, hollow wooden horse and hide in it with some soldiers.'

Odysseus beamed with pride.

'Then the rest of the Greek army pretended to go away and leave the horse as a gift to the Trojans. They wheeled the horse into the city and had a big party 'cos they thought the siege was over. Then at night, when all the Trojans were sleeping, him and the Greek soldiers jumped out of the horse, surprised everyone and captured Troy.'

Perce, Andy and Eddie stared in amazement at this outpouring of knowledge from Well'ard. This was surely a once-in-a-lifetime experience!

'How do YOU know, Well'ard?' asked Andy, awestruck. 'You shouldn't know about things like that. You never listen in class.'

'He's never IN class,' corrected Perce.

Eddie nodded agreement. 'You don't read and you only watch game shows!'

Well'ard looked hurt. 'Surprising the enemy. It's a military trick. The sort of thing I'll need to know when I'm in the SAS.'

Perce groaned. Of course! It was too much to expect that Well'ard would know about Greek mythology just for the joy of learning.

'So, what happened next?' asked Perce. 'Well'ard?'

'Dunno,' grunted Well'ard. 'The war bit ended, so I ain't bothered about the rest!'

Odysseus sighed. 'I began to try and get back home to Ithaca and my wife Penelope and son Telemachus, but I have had many misfortunes. No sooner had I left Troy . . .'

As the story of Odysseus's voyages unfolded, Perce and the others forgot the hard pebbles and the drizzle. They sat spellbound as he told them of the island where a one-eyed monster, the cyclops Polyphemus, had shut the hero and his men in a cave and begun eating them one by one. Odysseus had escaped by blinding the monster and hiding under the bellies of Polyphemus's sheep as they left the cave. Then he had reached the island of Aeolus, Keeper of the Winds . . .

'Keeper of the what?' asked Perce.

'Aeolus gave me the world's four winds in a bag, to help blow my ship home. But later we were attacked by . . . er . . .' Odysseus suddenly looked uncomfortable '. . . er . . . pirates, and my men opened the bag, hoping for a

14

wind to blow us to safety. Instead, the South Wind escaped and a mighty storm blew upon us. That is the last thing I remember before I found myself on the shores of your country.'

'Let's get this straight.' Perce spoke very slowly and calmly. 'This bloke gave you all the winds . . . in a *bag*?'

'Yes,' said Odysseus simply. He reached into the folds of his cloak and pulled out a salt-stained leather bag.

'I have them here.'

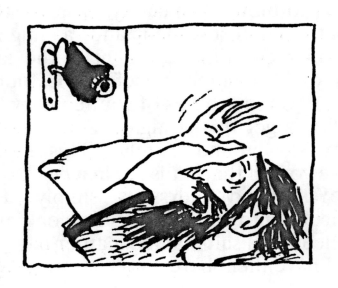

CHAPTER THREE

OL' ONE EYE IS BACK

'We can't just leave him here on the beach.' Perce bit her knuckles in concentration.

'Why not?' demanded Andy. 'Can't he look after himself?'

'Does it look like it?'

Odysseus sat huddled in his wet cloak, hugging his bag, looking the picture of misery. His teeth were chattering.

'Oh, great,' said Andy bitterly. 'It's bad enough things coming out of

Greek myths trying to do 'orrible things to us, now we're supposed to be *responsible* for them as well?'

Perce ignored him. 'We'll have to get him some clothes.'

'How are we supposed to do that? Wander into Top Bloke and ask 'em to kit him out in whatever the Well-Dressed Greek Hero is wearing this year?'

Well'ard looked puzzled. 'Why not?'

'Because he's not wearing proper clothes or shoes or anything, *and* he's soaking wet, *and* he's carrying a socking great sword, *and* . . . we haven't got any money.'

Well'ard sneered. 'I've got money.'

Perce stared at him. 'Are you saying we can use your money to buy clothes?'

'I didn't say you could use it, I just said I'd got it.'

Perce nodded. In spite of coming from a background so deprived that social workers invited each other round to see it, Well'ard always had money. He never seemed to spend it, he just had it.

'We could pinch some clothes off a

17

washing-line,' suggested Eddie.

Perce waved irritably at the dripping landscape and rain-lashed sea. 'Who'd be mad enough to dry clothes in this weather?'

'Anyway, that'd be stealin',' said Well'ard primly.

'Since when did that bother you?' Perce snorted. 'If you ever got on *Mastermind*, you'd do 'Nicking Things' as your Specialist Subject.'

Well'ard looked hurt. 'Ackcherly, I was going to say we could get him a tracksuit. From the Centre.'

Perce had to agree that this made sense. And it wasn't really stealing, any more than they'd stolen the tracksuits they were wearing. They'd just be borrowing it, and when they'd finished with it . . . whenever that was . . . they could give it back.

'There's another thing,' she said. 'We can smuggle him into the hostel if he's wearing a tracksuit.'

Andy was aghast. 'Into *our* hostel?'

'Well, he's got to stay somewhere.'

Well'ard tapped the shivering hero on the shoulder. 'C'mon, me old

China, we're off.'

Odysseus staggered to his feet and croaked, 'Whither?'

'What?'

'He means, where are we going?' explained Eddie.

Well'ard gave a grotesque wink. 'Never mind. Trust me.'

*   *   *

They wandered past the shuttered amusements on the sea front. It had taken some fast talking to persuade Odysseus to enter the 'great city', as he put it, of Bogmouth-on-Sylt. Evidently, the cities of his time had been smaller than most present-day towns.

When the first car had trundled along the promenade, he'd asked what it was. Eddie had told him it was a horseless chariot. Odysseus had shrugged and taken no more notice of the occasional traffic. Perce had been surprised by this, and said so to Andy.

'He doesn't seem to realize he's travelled three thousand years into the future.'

'Why should he? He's used to strange lands. I suppose, when you live in a place where there are all sorts of monsters like gorgons and fire-breathing bulls, and when you've built a wooden horse big enough to hide an army, the odd Volkswagen doesn't seem like too much of a big deal.'

'I suppose it's easier not to tell him about the time-travel bit.'

Turning into the driveway of the Outward Bound Centre, they slunk through the dripping bushes until they had a good view of the sports hall.

'They keep the tracksuits in there,' said Eddie, 'in the kit store. I had to take some back yesterday from the laundry.'

Perce turned to Well'ard. When pinching things was involved, he was the boss. 'What do we do now? Just walk in and grab a trackie?'

'I don't think so.' Well'ard was scanning the building critically.

'Why not?'

'*That's* why not.' Well'ard pointed to a corner of the building.

A security camera was mounted high

on the wall. As they watched, it swept jerkily across the face of the sports hall. A large notice underneath it proclaimed:

These premises are protected by Polyphemus Security Inc.

'Well, scratch that idea then,' said Andy. 'We'll have to think of something . . .' He suddenly became aware that Odysseus had become very still; he was staring at the camera and breathing heavily.

'That thing . . .' Odysseus licked his salt-dried lips. 'Can it see? Is it an eye?'

'Well, yes, sort of—' Eddie got no further.

Odysseus was shaking with fury. 'A cyclops!' The hero ground his teeth. 'Once more, a cyclops stands between me and safety.'

'It's not a—' Eddie began, but he was talking to thin air. Odysseus had vanished into the bushes. 'Hey, wait!'

Eddie scrambled off in pursuit. Perce and Andy followed him. 'Some hero!

Scared of a security camera.'

'I don't think he's scared.' They broke out of the bushes facing the sports field.

'What's he doing now?' asked Eddie.

Odysseus was striding over to a pile of equipment some thoughtful instructor had obviously laid out for the next session. He looked round, then picked up a javelin.

'Ooer.' Well'ard had joined them. 'What's he going to do with that?'

'He's not going to stick that thing in us, is he?' squeaked Eddie, going a funny colour.

'Hard to say,' muttered Perce. 'You know how Greeks like kebabs.'

They scattered as Odysseus strode towards them, but the hero ignored them, and pushed back through the bushes. Without a word they all followed.

They found Odysseus crouching behind a bush, fingering the javelin. The lens of the camera swept round, searching them out. As it pointed directly towards them, Odysseus leapt up and in the same movement wound back his arm and hurled the javelin. It barely curved as it cut through the air and smashed straight into the lens. A shower of blue sparks erupted from the camera as it jerked to a stop.

Well'ard looked up at Odysseus and whistled in awe. 'Double top,' he whispered. 'Played for and got!'

CHAPTER FOUR

BLOWN AWAY

'What are we going to do about him?' hissed Andy to Perce as he watched Odysseus pull on a tracksuit over his tunic.

Perce shrugged. 'I haven't got a clue.'

Odysseus finished zipping up the 'borrowed' tracksuit and picked up his sword and Bag of Winds.

Perce looked at them in alarm. 'You can't wander around Bogmouth with that sword, and we're supposed to put

24

bags in the locker-room. You'll have to leave them here.'

Odysseus shook his head and hugged the sword and bag to his chest. 'I will not surrender these. The sword is my faithful companion and Aeolus gave me the winds.'

'Lots of things give me the wind,' Eddie said quickly. He wasn't the sort to lose the opportunity for an obvious joke. 'F'r instance . . . cola . . . lemonade . . . baked beans . . .'

'All right, Eddie—' Perce tried to shut him up.

' . . . curry . . . pot noodles . . . Brussels sprouts.'

'EDDIE! We don't want to know about your bowels, thank you!' Perce turned back to Odysseus. 'All right, keep them, but you can't let the sword be seen. Hide it.'

Odysseus nodded his agreement and tucked the sword down his left trouser leg.

'What now?' asked Andy.

'Let's get back to the dormitories before anybody sees us and wonders why we've finished the orienteering so quickly,' answered Perce. 'Come on.'

Well'ard checked that the way was clear and quickly beckoned the group out of the kit store. They sprinted across the courtyard towards the Centre's accommodation block. Odysseus limped after them, the sword down his leg causing him to hop like Long John Silver.

'Hugh lot! Where do you think hugh are going?' A voice boomed across the courtyard.

The group came to a sudden stop and slowly turned to face Sergeant-Major Ron Eisenhower, leader of the Outward Bound Centre.

He marched over to the group and eyed them suspiciously. 'What are hugh doing back so hearly? Hugh began the horienteering course at oh-sevener-hundred hours. Hit should have taken hugh a-three and a half hours. Hit is now oh-niner-thirty hours. Hugh are sixty minutes too hearly! H-why?'

Having been released from thirty years in the army, Sergeant-Major Eisenhower had decided that he still wanted to boss people around and so

26

he'd set up an Outward Bound Centre where he could shout at people to his heart's content.

He was known to the kids as Major Eyeswater after an incident involving Eddie on the first day of the course.

The group had been taken abseiling. This involved being strapped into a climbing harness, stepping backwards over a cliff face and walking down it slowly.

As the Sergeant-Major explained the procedure, Eddie whispered to Perce: 'You'd have to be crazy to do that.'

'So who would like to go first?' asked the Sergeant-Major.

Perce decided to 'volunteer' Eddie.

'Eddie will,' yelled out Perce.

Eddie's jaw dropped. 'Why me?' he hissed at Perce.

' 'Cos you are crazy,' she smiled sweetly.

'Gude man,' beamed the Sergeant-Major as he bundled the protesting Eddie into the climbing harness.

As he stepped backwards over the cliff, Eddie managed somehow to get the climbing rope caught between his legs. He panicked, grabbed the rope and began to shoot down the cliff face. The climbing rope snaked through his crotch and Eddie clamped his legs tight round it to slow his speedy descent. Friction between rope and trousers caused overheating of Eddie's nether regions. Black smoke began shooting out from his flies, and his eyes streamed with tears.

After that episode, the Sergeant-Major became known as Major Eyeswater, in honour of Eddie and his burning crotch.

Now the Sergeant-Major stood before them, staring at Odysseus.

'Who's this, then?'

'Er . . . new kid.' Years of telling porkies had given Well'ard lightning reflexes where lying was concerned. 'Came this morning.'

Major Eyeswater seemed to accept Well'ard's story. This was strange, as Odysseus had a beard and was clearly at least thirty years older than any other kid on the course. Perce had never quite worked out what happened when other people saw the mythological visitors she and Andy attracted, but she was pretty sure they didn't see what she saw.

Major Eyeswater humphed. 'He doesn't say much, does he? What's his h-name?'

'Odysse*ooer* . . . I mean . . . er . . . Otis Hughes.' Well'ard's brain was running on turbo.

'*Hotis*?' The Sergeant-Major looked suspiciously at Well'ard, not knowing whether to believe him. 'H-are you having me hon, laddie? Why have hugh got a stupid grin hon your face?'

'Because he's stupid,' Perce answered. Well'ard turned and scowled.

'Well, seeing hugh are back so hearly, hugh can do a couple of laps of the hassault course to fill in time.'

Andy groaned. 'Couldn't we fill in time by having a cup of tea and watching the telly?'

'Certainly not! Hugh are here to henjoy yourselves,' boomed the Sergeant-Major. 'You cannot henjoy yourself watching television!'

29

'We could give it a try . . .' mumbled Andy.

'No. The hassault course—*that's* hentertainment. Hoff hugh go and . . .' The Sergeant-Major stopped and stared quizzically at Odysseus. 'What's that necklace hugh are wearing, lad?' He pointed at the Bag of Winds dangling from Odysseus's neck. 'Hugh can't go on the hassault course with a necklace. Give it to me.' He marched across to Odysseus and grabbed the bag from the startled hero.

'No, you shall not have them!'

Perce stared in horror as Odysseus reached into the depths of the tracksuit for his sword. How would they explain one skewered Outward Bound instructor? Luckily for the Sergeant-Major, Odysseus couldn't get his sword out; instead he lunged towards the bag.

'What do hugh think hugh h-are doing?'

As the Sergeant-Major and Odysseus struggled, Perce's eyes were drawn to the bag. It seemed to her to inflate and then deflate in a steady rhythm. Almost as if it's breathing, she thought.

Then the bag began to billow and seemed to expand to near bursting point. At that moment Odysseus managed to wrestle the bag from Eisenhower. However, the Sergeant-Major had years of single-combat training experience. He held on to the drawstring of the bag and yanked it hard. The neck of the bag spilled open.

'Ha!' exclaimed the Sergeant-Major in triumph. Odysseus saw what was happening and tried to pull the drawstring tight. He was too late. There was an ear-splitting, gut-wrenching roar as a blast of ice-cold wind burst from the bag and enveloped the Sergeant-Major in a buffeting, raging and twisting torrent of air.

The Sergeant-Major dropped the drawstring and cried out in astonishment: 'Blow me backwards!'

And the wind did just that. Blew him backwards, sideways and finally upwards in a spiralling tornado.

As Odysseus pounced on the bag and closed it, Andy, Perce, Well'ard and Eddie shielded their faces from the blast and tried to look heavenwards at the rapidly disappearing instructor.

Then, as quickly as it started, the roaring and pounding ceased. The air became calm and still as leaves and bits of paper fluttered back to the ground.

The four kids stood blinking. The Sergeant-Major was nowhere to be seen.

CHAPTER FIVE

CONSULTING THE ORACLE

Perce led the way into the TV lounge
and flopped into a grubby chair.

'Now what?' Eddie ran trembling
fingers through his hair.

Perce bit her lip and shrugged.

'Don't just sit there! We've got to
bring him back!'

Perce glared at Eddie. 'Got any
bright ideas about how we do that?'
Eddie subsided. 'Me neither. So, let's
try just sitting and thinking for a bit.'

Well'ard grunted. Thinking wasn't

33

his strong point; he mooched over to the TV Perce heard him switch the set on.

Andy spread his hands helplessly. 'But where did he go?'

Odysseus's deep voice answered solemnly, 'To the back of the North Wind.'

'We know that,' snapped Perce, 'we saw him. He must have gone *miles* . . .'

Andy was staring at Odysseus. 'I don't think he means . . . what's wrong with him?'

At the first buzz of sound from the TV set, Odysseus had pricked his ears; as the picture wavered into life, he stared, transfixed, at the screen. He cocked his head to one side, like a dog that isn't sure what to do. Eddie started to giggle.

Odysseus seemed to come to a decision. He dragged the sword from his tracksuit, and raised it over the television.

'Nooooo!' Perce, Andy and Eddie threw themselves on Odysseus and tried to wrestle the sword from him, while Well'ard, horror-stricken, spread himself in front of the threatened TV set like a mother defending her baby.

Even as they struggled, Perce realized that Odysseus could have flung them off easily; he was trying not to hurt them.

'Why do you prevent me?' he panted.

'Leave it alone! What are you *doing*?'

'There are people . . . imprisoned . . . in that box . . .'

'Stop! Listen, please! It's not how it looks.' Odysseus stopped struggling, but didn't take his eyes off the TV screen. Perce held on to his sword arm, just in case. 'They're not really in there. It's just a box . . . with pictures . . . a sort of viewer . . .' Perce struggled to find words that would mean something to the hero '. . . It shows you things that are happening far away . . .'

Odysseus relaxed suddenly and nodded. 'An oracle.'

Perce wasn't sure about this, but she wasn't going to argue. 'Right.'

Odysseus, without taking his eyes off the screen, sat down next to Well'ard and watched the flickering images.

Andy breathed a sigh of relief.

'I wish he'd stop *doing* things like that,' Eddie complained, massaging a sore arm.

Perce turned to Andy. 'What did you mean when you said he didn't mean what I thought he meant?'

'What? Oh . . .' Andy rewound the conversation in his head. ' "Back of the North Wind", yeah. I don't think he just meant "a long way away". I think he meant *really* at the back of the North Wind . . . wherever that is.'

It took some time to attract Odysseus's attention; he seemed to be mesmerized by the television. When he understood the question, he confirmed that Major Eyeswater, on opening the Bag of Winds, had been blown away by the North Wind.

'How can you tell it was the North Wind?' asked Perce.

Odysseus shrugged and kept his eyes on the screen.

Eddie said, 'I suppose he thinks that's a daft question. It's like asking us how we know the carpet in here is blue.

We know it's blue because it's blue.'

Andy nodded. 'He said his sailors let loose the South Wind which blew him up here, then Major Eyeswater opened the bag and released the North Wind. So, now there should just be the East and West Winds left in the bag.'

Perce shook her head in bafflement. 'Is that supposed to make sense?'

'Wonderful!' Odysseus was glued to an advert for toilet paper. 'I like this story about the little puppy. What is he running away with?'

*　　　*　　　*

The morning wore on. Perce argued fiercely that the whole situation was totally unreal. Her position was slightly undermined by the very solid bulk of Odysseus, who sat gazing at the TV screen and munching his way through packets of crisps from the vending machine in the corridor.

Eventually, Perce pulled up a chair to one side of Odysseus.

'You like television, do you?'

Odysseus nodded dreamily. *'Wizzo*

37

washes whiter,' he crooned.

'Good.' Perce nodded to Andy. The screen went dead.

'Make it come back!' Odysseus jabbed frantically at the remote control, to no avail. Andy had switched the set off at the wall.

Perce shook her head. 'Not until you tell us how we get the Sergeant-Major back.'

Odysseus waved his arms in exasperation. 'I don't know! You must consult the oracle.' He indicated the TV.

Perce stared at him. 'It doesn't work that way. It's just a TV.'

'The voice of the gods.' Odysseus was feeling the set all over, trying to get it to work.

'It isn't! You can't ask it questions or anything!'

Odysseus shrugged. 'Some oracles are like that. You just have to listen for the part of the prophecy that concerns you.'

Unexpectedly, Eddie agreed. 'Might as well. You never know, the Sergeant-Major might be on the news.

"Raving Mad Instructor Lands at North Pole"—or something.'

Perce waved her arm wearily. 'Oh, turn it on!'

As the TV came back to life, a pulsating rock rhythm blasted from a female vocal group. Odysseus sat bolt upright. To Perce's amusement, as the pictures appeared on the screen, the hero began jigging in time to the beat.

'Hey, the Sirens!' Well'ard yelled his approval. 'They're wicked!'

'Wicked?' A look of puzzlement crossed Odysseus's face. 'These women are evil?'

Perce grinned. 'He means they're good.'

'**Hear the fabulous sound of the Sirens— LIVE!**' roared the voice-over. '**Now on tour coast-to-coast in the UK . . .**'

The tour dates appeared on the screen. Well'ard let out a whoop. 'Hey, dudes! They're here! In Bogmouth! Tonight!'

The screen switched to a weather map. Perce turned the sound down. 'Never mind the Sirens. We've got to find a way of getting Odysseus back.'

Odysseus dragged his gaze from the TV screen and stared at Perce in amazement.

'In Athene's name, what makes you think I want to go back?'

CHAPTER SIX

OTIS HUGHES, GO HOME!

Perce was horrified. 'You've *got* to go back.'

Odysseus folded his arms and looked mulish. 'Shan't.'

'But . . . but . . . what about your family? They need you.'

'Ha!' Odysseus glared at her. 'You don't know my family. Take my son Telemachus . . . a right little tearaway, he is. Never listens to a word I say. And as for my dear wife Penelope . . . well, I left home years ago. I suppose she thinks I'm dead. I bet she married the first man who came along.'

Perce remembered this bit of the story. Penelope had attracted many admirers, but she told them she had to do her weaving before she would choose one. She undid at night all the work she had done during the day, so she never finished it.

Perce had never been able to believe that Penelope was such a wimp. Why didn't she just tell all those blokes to get lost? She told Odysseus how his wife kept her suitors at bay.

'I'm not surprised,' Odysseus muttered darkly. 'She tried that one on me a few times.' He gave Perce a suspicious look. 'Anyway, how do you know?'

'I . . . er . . . heard.' It wouldn't help the situation if Odysseus discovered he was not only a thousand miles from home, but three thousand years as well. 'Gossip. You know how it is.'

Andy waded in at this point with an appeal to Odysseus's patriotism. How did he think Greece would get along without the man who won the Trojan

War?

Odysseus replied that the Trojan War would never have started in the first place if King Menelaus of Sparta ('silly old fool') hadn't married a woman young enough to be his daughter . . .

Eddie nodded. 'Helen. The Most Beautiful Woman in the World . . .'

'So she kept telling us. Well, was that asking for trouble or what? Prince Paris, Mister Too-Gorgeous-To-Live, comes along and whisks Helen off to Troy.' Odysseus snorted. 'Ten years of bloodshed over that stupid girl and her fool of a boyfriend. And now, Zeus knows how, I find myself in a land of miracles!' He gestured at the TV set. 'Horseless chariots, great ships that move without sails or oars, huge metal birds . . .' Odysseus's face took on a look of ecstasy '. . . boxes that keep things cool, magic food in pots . . . just add boiling water . . .'

'Are you telling me', shrieked Perce, 'that you want to stay here because of *Pot Noodles*?'

'. . . and you would have me leave

this wonderful new world and send me back into the clutches of Circe?' Odysseus stopped suddenly. He looked down at his feet.

Aha, thought Perce. 'Who's this Circe, then?' she asked sweetly.

Odysseus stared at the floor. 'Mutter mutter.'

'Sounds like a girl's name. Circe's a girl, is she?'

'Muttermutter.' Odysseus rubbed his hands together and crossed his feet. The back of his neck went all pink.

Oho! thought Perce. 'Ran out on her, did you?'

'She is a foul witch!' roared Odysseus, springing to his feet.

Any excuse, thought Perce. 'Right, right,' she said soothingly.

'She turned my men into pigs!'

Perce thought most men *were* pigs, but with Odysseus having a wobbler with a sharp sword to hand, it didn't seem a good moment to say so.

'So, you got out as quick as you could, right?'

'Well, I had to stay for a *bit* . . .' Odysseus looked sheepish. 'She said she'd turn my men back, but it took time for the spell to wear off. And one thing led to another and we had three sons, but—'

'*Three?*' squeaked Perce.

'—but then I said I ought to be going home, and she was just totally unreasonable! Wouldn't let me go! She chased me, and that's when my men opened the Bag of Winds . . .'

'But you said you were attacked by pirates!' objected Perce.

'Oh, did I?' said Odysseus, unconvincingly. 'Anyway, if you think I'm going back to be chased across the world by a mad witch, you are mistaken. No way, horsie!'

'That's *José*,' corrected Eddie.

The arrival of the rest of the orienteering group, steaming slightly, put an end to the debate. Perce glared at Odysseus, who folded his arms and looked defiant.

*   *   *

At lunch, the Outward Bound instructors were clearly puzzled by

Major Eyeswater's disappearance, but they couldn't admit they didn't know what was going on and it simply never occurred to them to ask the kids if anyone knew where the Sergeant-Major was. At any rate, Perce was relieved to find that she, Andy, Eddie and Well'ard wouldn't have to face a barrage of questions. For the rest of the day, activities went on as normal with a programme of sports.

It wasn't long before 'Otis Hughes' was causing a sensation. He was useless at any ball game, but in all the other activities he was in a class of his own. In archery, every arrow hit the gold centre of the target. He could hurl a javelin twice as far as any of the instructors, and a discus clear out of sight. Unwisely, one of the instructors tried to teach Odysseus the art of self-defence. After wrestling with the hero, the poor man felt so faint he had to go and have a lie-down.

After supper, Odysseus was the centre of attention in the TV lounge, and was clearly enjoying himself. Perce beckoned Andy, Eddie and Well'ard to join her in the corridor.

'He's got to go!' she hissed savagely. 'Before he blows anybody else away.'

'Fine, but how do we get rid of him?' Andy shrugged.

'We could tell the police,' suggested Eddie.

'Or the SAS,' added Well'ard. The others groaned.

'That won't do any good. Nobody will notice anything wrong. Look at our lot and the instructors. He just looks like another kid to them.'

This was true. Odysseus's sudden appearance hadn't caused so much as a raised eyebrow.

'Sooner or later somebody's going to notice something,' Andy pointed out, 'especially if he sticks a javelin in someone.'

'The Bag of Winds!' Perce clicked her fingers as inspiration struck. 'One wind blew him here, so another one could blow him back!'

'That's a thought.' Andy's face clouded. 'How do we get hold of the bag?'

Well'ard was scornful. 'We nick it,

div. We go back in there, you three keep him talking, I grab the bag and Ah, Bisto!'

'Hey presto,' corrected Eddie.

'Yeah, that an' all.'

It was a good plan, and it might have worked but for one small thing. When they got back to the TV lounge, Odysseus had disappeared.

CHAPTER SEVEN

SIREN SONG

Perce flung herself at the kid sitting nearest the door. 'Where is he?'

The kid looked at her in astonishment. 'Who?'

'Odysse . . . Otis Hughes . . . the new guy!'

'Oh, him!' The kid shrugged. 'He went out.'

'I can see that, you dingbat. When?'

'Few minutes ago. He was watching telly and then he suddenly started jigging about like he'd got a wasp up his trousers, then he looked all weird, like this.' The kid did a passable imitation of a zombie.

'What was he watching?'

'That Sirens advert was on, I think . . . you know, for the concert tonight.'

Andy clicked his fingers. 'He did that when that advert came on before, remember? That must be where he's gone.'

Perce shook her head to clear it. 'Let's get this straight. Odysseus gets blown three thousand years into the future and the first thing he does is decide to go to a *rock concert*?!' She headed for the door.

'Where are you going?'

'Where do you think? To get him back!'

*   *   *

'There he is!'

It hadn't been difficult to sneak out of the hostel. The instructors were too busy searching for Major Eyeswater to keep a close watch on the kids. Perce, with Andy, Well'ard and Eddie in tow, had pounded down the promenade towards the Pavilion Theatre on the sea front. They arrived in the foyer just in time to see an usher ask Odysseus for his ticket. Odysseus turned and saw Perce and her friends. He fixed the unfortunate usher with a look that would have melted a marble slab.

'They have it.'

Giving the usher no time to recover, he turned on his heel and marched into the theatre.

Perce and the others made to follow, only to be stopped by the usher, who was in no mood to take any messing about from a bunch of kids. 'He says you've got his ticket. Where is it? Where're yours, come to that?'

Perce glared at him. 'You don't understand! We've got to get in there and find him. It's important.'

The usher scowled. 'You can get in there when I see your tickets.'

'Hang on!' Perce turned and dragged the others into a corner. 'It's no good, they won't let us in without a ticket. I haven't got any money. What about you?' Andy and Eddie shook their heads.

They all turned to look at Well'ard.

'No chance!' Well'ard was scornful. 'Think I'm going to buy you lot tickets to get in there? In your dreams!'

Perce gave him her very sweetest smile. She knew something about Well'ard she'd been saving up to use as blackmail. Now seemed a good time.

'Yes, you will.'

'Yeah? Why?'

'Because I know how you get your money.' Well'ard jumped as if he'd been shot. For a moment he looked scared, then he rallied.

'You don't. You're just saying that. I don't believe you.'

Perce's voice was candy-floss soft. 'Buy those tickets, or I shall say the b-word.'

Well'ard turned white. His eyes bulged. 'Not the b-word,' he croaked. Andy and Eddie regarded him in amazement.

'Buy the tickets.' Perce smirked in triumph as Well'ard, shoulders slumped in defeat, slouched back to the box office.

*　　　*　　　*

The hall was packed. Most days it was used for dances by the blue-rinsed ravers among Bogmouth's senior citizens. The dance-floor was now covered with a swaying mass of fans all straining to see the stage. The sweaty darkness was hotter than a greenhouse in hell.

'We'll never spot him from down here!' Perce glanced around. 'Come on!' She led the way to the balcony that ran around three sides of the hall. Pushing through the crowds with Andy, she signalled Well'ard (who was still moaning about the cost of the tickets) and Eddie to go to the opposite side. She shoved her way to the front of the balcony and scanned the mob below anxiously as the PA system screeched into life.

'**Ladeeze an' Gennlemen,**' howled a voice, '**are you ready to get down to the hottest sound around? Let's hear it for . . . the Sirens.**'

The lights on the stage flicked off.

The applause faded uncertainly in the total darkness, to be replaced by the eerie far-off wailing of a police siren. Blue flashing lights swept the crowd. In one flash, Perce caught a glimpse of Odysseus's tracksuited figure. She grabbed Andy's arm and pointed as the wailing built up to a cacophony of ear-melting noise.

Bright lights hammered on to the stage, and the Sirens began their act. They were dressed in shimmering silver jumpsuits that looked as if they'd been put on with a spray can. The audience howled its delight as they sang the opening number:

'Listen to the cry of shipwrecked souls . . .'

They strutted about the stage together. There was something snakelike in their movement—supple, smooth and dangerous. Perce turned to Andy, whose eyes were riveted on the stage. His lips formed words that looked suspiciously like 'Babe-tastic'! Perce kicked him savagely on the shin.

'As the ocean sucks them down . . .'

The lead singer wore a gold mask. She kept to the front of the stage, reaching down to (but never quite touching) the outstretched hands of the audience.

'So tie yourself to the mast, now, honey . . .'

Perce caught sight of Odysseus. He was moving forward through the dense mass of bodies like a man in a trance, his gaze fixed on the lead singer, until he stood at the foot of the stage face to face with the golden mask.

' 'Cos if you hear me callin' you, you're gonna drown!'

The lead singer reached up and whipped aside her mask. There was a moment of complete silence. Everyone in the hall heard Odysseus scream one word: *'Circe!'*

He turned and began to fight his way back through the crowd, whose angry yells gave way to screams as the other Sirens changed. Their fingernails became claws, their hair grew wild and ragged, and their teeth . . . Perce turned away.

Howling, Odysseus hurled himself at the exit. With a screech of triumph, Circe and the Sirens plunged from the stage in pursuit.

CHAPTER EIGHT

MAKIN' BACON

'Follow him!' Perce cried out to the others as she ran towards the stairs. 'Don't let him get away.'

'Why not?' asked Andy as the kids charged past shocked bouncers and down the stairs. 'At least if they get hold of him he'll be off our hands.'

Well'ard and Eddie joined them in the foyer as Perce faced up to Andy. 'Then what? . . . What happens about Circe and the others? You know the sort of things mythological monsters can do.'

Andy, Eddie and Well'ard remembered things that had happened to them. They shivered.

'So, we've got to find him. Now, come on!' They rushed out of the theatre into the October night air. There was no sign of Odysseus or his pursuers.

'Where could they be?' asked Perce. Andy and Eddie shrugged.

'If I was hiding from someone, I'd choose somewhere dark.' Well'ard was the expert in running away and hiding from people. 'There!'

Well'ard pointed towards the pier standing opposite the theatre. The Victorian pier was Bogmouth's only claim to fame. In the summer it was a hive of activity, with its amusement arcades, sweet stalls, sideshows and even a funfair. But now, with the season just ended, the deserted pier stood unlit and brooding, jutting out into the sea.

'Are you sure?' asked Andy. 'It's very dark.'

'Scared of the dark, wimp?' snarled

Well'ard.

'No, I'm scared of the things that can hide in the dark, leap out at you, and rip your head off,' replied Andy.

Perce ignored Andy. 'We're going in!'

*   *   *

They climbed over the locked gates, and crept past the silent arcades into the funfair. At every scuffling sound they stopped and peered into the gloom. Andy and Eddie were both hoping that Odysseus hadn't tried to hide on the pier and Well'ard had made a mistake. Although he'd never have admitted it, so was Well'ard.

Perce looked up at the twisting silhouette of the roller-coaster. She read its peeling sign:

Monster Splash

'Monsters everywhere you look,' she hissed. Andy's reply was lost as a loud screeching sound made the kids jump. They blinked like startled rabbits before Perce recovered her wits. 'Hide!'

The four kids ran to the entrance of the roller-coaster and dived into two of the dragon-shaped cars.

Out of the gloom, the figure of Circe appeared. The Sirens trailed after her, sniffing the air like hounds searching for a scent. Their reptilian green eyes pierced the darkness.

'Odysseus! My love, my sweet, my precious,' cooed Circe. 'I'm here for you, my darling. Where are you?'

Perce peered over the dragon's tail to see what was coming next.

Blue sparks of electricity sparked and crackled from Circe's hands. With an ear-piercing zap, bolts of lightning forked out from her fingertips, shooting around the fairground. Neon lights every colour of the rainbow fizzed and blinked on, lighting up the pier.

Andy sat hunched and shaking in his car.

'She's turned on all the lights!' Perce cried in disbelief.

Well'ard grabbed the neck of the

dragon in which he and Eddie were crouched. 'And the rides! We're moving— strap yourselves in!'

Eddie's stomach shot into his mouth as the dragon cars began to move. 'I hate things like this,' he wailed. 'I get sick!'

Suddenly Odysseus leapt up from his hiding-place in the leading car. 'Begone, foul demon!' he cried, shaking his fist at Circe, before the accelerating ride forced him back into his seat.

With a cry of joy, Circe and the Sirens sprang into the cars behind the kids.

'I'm here, lover,' crooned the witch.

'Go away!' Odysseus's yell was lost as his dragon began plummeting down and around the track. Eddie clapped a hand to his mouth.

For the next few seconds everything was a blur. Wind rushed through the kids' hair as they were buffeted and flung around.

'Oh no!' squealed Eddie.

The track plunged down a near-vertical slope. The kids screamed as the dragons roared on at breakneck speed. Circe, defying gravity, stood in her car, arms outstretched, pleading with Odysseus.

'Come to me, my—'

SPLASH!

At that moment, Odysseus's car ploughed through a water-trough. The kids ducked as a wall of water shot over their heads and hit the witch smack in the face. Circe staggered to her feet, dripping and coughing. Her hair hung in rats' tails.

Odysseus turned to face her, sword in hand.

'Leave me be!' he shouted. 'I don't love you!'

Circe flinched. Her lips pursed. Her voice was a rasp. 'Is this how you repay my love? NOBODY TREATS ME LIKE THAT!'

Perce glanced back. She could see blue sparks flame from Circe's fingers. Uh oh! she thought. Here's trouble.

A bolt of energy shot from Circe's fingers and headed towards Odysseus. Just at that moment, Odysseus's car sped over a hump in the track. Perce and Andy's car followed. As they raced down the dip, there was a great flash of blue light behind them.

Perce gasped in dismay. 'Well'ard! Eddie!'

To her relief, Well'ard and Eddie's car shot over the rise. At the same moment the cars began to slow down as they neared the end of the ride.

As his car jerked to a halt, Odysseus vaulted over its side and sped away. Perce and Andy leapt out of their car and waited impatiently for Well'ard and Eddie. The third car juddered to rest.

'Well'ard! Eddie! Come on!' Perce glanced frantically back up the track. 'They'll be here in a minute!'

There was no movement from the car.

'Well'ard? Eddie?'

Andy reached out and wrenched open the door.

Well'ard and Eddie stood quivering from the tips of their moist snouts to their little pink trotters sticking out from Outward Bound tracksuits.

Andy gawped, horror-stricken. 'She's turned them into pigs!'

CHAPTER NINE

HICKS IN THE STYX

The squealing porkers exploded from the car and charged for shelter in the darkness behind some booths. Perce and Andy followed and crouched with their hearts in their mouths as the Sirens' cars reached the end of the ride. On Circe's signal, the creatures spread out and loped away to search the fairground.

The hunters faded into the shadows.

Andy shook his head in disbelief. 'She turned them into pigs!' he said again.

'How can you tell the difference?' snapped Perce.

'What are we going to do?' wailed Andy.

'Keep your voice down!' Perce peered cautiously round the side of a booth.

Andy was practically tearing his hair out. 'How can we get Major Eyeswater back, make Well'ard and Eddie human again . . .'

'What do you mean, "again"?' asked Perce acidly.

'. . . and get rid of Circe and the Sirens *and* Odysseus . . .?' Andy shook his head in despair.

'Groink!' A slobbery nose snuffled Perce's elbow.

Perce spun round. 'Get off!' She glared at the pig. It looked sheepish, which was difficult for a pig. But was it Well'ard, or Eddie?

The pig turned away and wolfed down a half-eaten beefburger someone had dropped weeks before.

'Oh, hi, Well'ard. Where's Eddie?'

'Greink!' Another pig stuck its pink

nose out from under a tarpaulin in a shadowy corner.

Andy gazed at the pigs in fascinated horror. 'So, what do we do next?'

'Oh, well, that's easy.' Perce's patience was at breaking-point. 'We go to the chemist's and get a bottle of Piggo, the wonder medicine, guaranteed to turn pigs to people—*how do I know what we do next*?!'

'Ssssssh!' Andy held an urgent finger to his lips.

'Don't you shush me! What makes you think—'

'There he is!'

Perce turned to follow Andy's pointing finger. Further down the pier, Odysseus was slinking from one shadow to the next.

'Come on.' Perce sneaked round the corner of the booth in pursuit, followed by Andy. A moment later, she peered back round the corner and beckoned.

'Groink!'

'Greink!'

Pig Well'ard and Pig Eddie backed into the darkest corner they could find. They didn't want to meet Circe again.

'Can you imagine what will happen to a couple of fat little piggies caught wandering round without an owner?' growled Perce. 'How about it? Wanna stay here—bacon features?' Perce ducked back round the corner.

Trotters scrabbling on the smooth planks, Pig Well'ard and Pig Eddie rushed to follow her.

*   *   *

They followed Odysseus down the line of rides and stalls. Twice they had to dive for cover as a Siren sped past, searching. They were sneaking down a passage between two rides when a hand shot out and clamped tight over Perce's mouth. She gave a muffled scream. Instantly, she felt Odysseus's sword at her throat.

'Silence!' Odysseus spun her round. 'Why do you follow me?'

'What d'you lot think you're doing?'

Perce and Andy spun round to see a policeman bearing down on them.

'That's all we need!' Perce grabbed Andy. 'Leg it!'

Odysseus had already dived for the nearest ride. Transparent spectres hovered over a graveyard scene in which skeletons and nastier things prowled.

'He's getting on the ghost train!' Perce and Andy skidded to a halt as Odysseus leapt into an empty car just as it slammed through the rubber doors and into the tunnel.

Behind them, the policeman yelled, ' 'Ere . . .'

Perce and Andy leapt into the next car as it shot forward. The policeman made a grab for them and missed. 'Hey!'

Two pigs shot through the policeman's legs and scrambled into the third car. He gawped at them in shock. 'Oi!'

'Groink!' corrected Pig Well'ard.

'Greink!' agreed Pig Eddie.

Their car trundled through the doors.

*   *   *

As they rode into the gloomy tunnel,

ducking plastic cobwebs, Perce and Andy heard a voice roaring defiance in the darkness before them. Rounding a bend, they were just in time to see a ghost pop out beside Odysseus's car with an eerie wail. A microsecond later, Odysseus's sword had sliced the fake spook in half.

'Ghosts!' thundered Odysseus, standing in his car and staring wildly about him. 'Furies . . . monsters . . . demons!'

A voice behind them roared, 'Stop!' Perce and Andy turned. Two pink snouts peered from the car behind theirs. The policeman was pounding along grimly in the rear. 'You're all under arrest!'

But Odysseus wasn't listening. Lights blazed, triggered by his car's arrival. A crypt appeared, a coffin creaked open, and Dracula with one fang missing sat up briefly before Odysseus leapt from his car and decapitated the vampire, which expired with a despairing squeak. Odysseus swung aboard Perce and Andy's car as it passed.

'It seems we have crossed the Styx

into Hades,' he snapped. 'By some magic of Circe's, we have been sent to the Underworld.'

'No, you don't understand!' yelled Perce. 'It's not—'

A moth-eaten Frankenstein's monster rose from its slab with a shuddering groan. With a howl of rage, Odysseus charged, sending the polystyrene creature slamming into the wall. The thin plywood shattered under the weight; Odysseus and the dummy tumbled through into the night air. Perce and Andy baled out of their car and followed.

'At last!'

Odysseus, Perce and Andy spun round in horror. Circe stepped out of the shadows and halted before the jagged gap in the plywood. As they stood transfixed, the witch raised her hand. Power began to crackle from her fingers. Two pink torpedoes pelted through the hole behind Circe, slamming into her legs. She shot into the air with a screech.

The two pigs sprinted past Perce. Circe fell backwards just as the luckless

70

policeman stuck his head through the gap in the ghost-train wall. Her spell caught him right between the eyes.

'All right now,' he said, 'let's be having yo*oooink*!' His voice rose to a squeal and his snout quivered as he watched Perce, Andy and Odysseus dash off after the two porkers.

The policeman shook his head sadly. His little pink tail drooped. It had been a pig of a day.

CHAPTER TEN

THE END-OF-THE-PIER SHOW

Leaving the funfair behind, Perce and Andy raced seawards along the empty, windswept pier with Pig Well'ard and Pig Eddie clattering at their heels. Odysseus had outpaced them, pounding ahead, but suddenly he stopped and gazed around frantically. A moment later, Perce realized why.

They had reached the end of the pier. There was nowhere left to run. Below them, water as black as oil sucked and gurgled around ironwork that glinted in the pale moonlight.

Perce swung round to face Odysseus. 'So, what do we do now, O great leader?'

He scowled at her. 'You have brought this end upon yourselves by following me.'

Perce clenched her fists. 'Oh really? We should have left you on the beach this morning? We should have let you roam around smashing things and blowing people away? And look what your girlfriend did to Well'ard and Eddie!' She advanced on the hero. 'You've caused enough trouble and you're not going to run out on us, not before you've put things right.'

Odysseus shook his head. 'Even if I were powerful enough to overcome Circe, I don't know of a way to change your friends back.'

'Then you'll have to find a way, because—'

There was a howl of triumph from behind them.

'The Sirens!' Odysseus grasped his sword, his face set. 'They have found our trail. We cannot go back.'

'Over here!' Andy beckoned furiously from the other side of the pier. He was scrabbling at the floor. 'There's a trapdoor here, but it won't budge.'

Odysseus stepped to Andy's side. He found the edge of the trapdoor, slipped the blade of his sword between it and the floor, and leaned on the hilt. Something snapped and with a creaking groan, the trapdoor opened. Perce stuck her head down the trap and gave a muffled cry of delight. 'Hey, whaddaya know! Pedalos!'

A rickety ladder led downwards. Under the pier was a sort of storeroom, or perhaps a boathouse. A single uncovered bulb flooded the space with dim yellow light. Ranged along the walls were stacked the double-hulled pedal boats that summer visitors hired from the small jetty at the end of the pier. This must be where they were stored for the winter.

'Come!' Odysseus grabbed Pig Eddie, tucked the astonished porker under one arm, and slid down the hole. Perce and Andy watched him descend the ladder one-handed. Another howl, sounding closer, made them start. Perce saw something move against the lights of the distant funfair. Odysseus's bearded face reappeared.

'Down you go. I will bring the other one.'

Wordlessly, Perce started down the ladder, followed by Andy. A few seconds later, they were joined by Odysseus carrying Pig Well'ard.

Perce stepped forward as Odysseus set down his struggling burden. 'Thanks.'

Odysseus bowed. 'You are right. I have brought much trouble on you. I will make what amends I can.'

Andy was tugging at the ropes holding the nearest pedalo in place. Perce looked around. 'There are doors over here, and a sort of ramp.'

'Slipway,' corrected Andy.

'Whatever. They must launch the boats down it.'

Odysseus's sword made short work of the padlock on the doors; Perce swung them open and peered down the slipway. 'It's not far to the water. It must be high tide.'

Odysseus eyed a pedalo dubiously. 'This is some kind of vessel?'

'It's a paddle-boat,' Perce explained. 'You sit *there* and push the pedals round with your feet and steer with that bar *there* and it goes.'

Odysseus shook his head. 'It doesn't look very seaworthy to me.'

'We don't have to sail the Seven Seas on it, just get away from here!'

With an abrupt nod, Odysseus put down his sword and held out the Bag of Winds to Perce. 'Hold this.' He tugged the nearest pedalo to the slipway. The twin hulls slotted neatly into runners, and the boat slid smoothly down the ramp. It met the water with a thunderous splash, and rode there rocking in the gentle swell.

Working frantically, Perce and Andy untied the second pedalo and Odysseus dragged it to the slipway. As they held it ready to launch, a hiss of triumph sounded from above their heads.

Perce looked up to see a Siren, eyes burning and teeth bared in a wicked grin, peering through the trap. The creature flung back its head and howled in triumph. A second and third head appeared, only to cringe away as Circe herself appeared and gazed down at them.

'Well, my little piglets,' she purred, 'nowhere left to run?'

She closed her eyes. Her lips moved. Once again, her arm lifted to fling a curse upon their heads.

Perce swung round. 'Incoming!' she yelled. 'Go!'

Three humans and two pigs leapt aboard the tiny craft as it bucketed down the slipway. Circe's spell detonated harmlessly in the deserted boathouse.

The impact with the water flung Perce overboard. She floundered over to the first pedalo and dragged herself aboard. A struggling pink shape, doing the piggy-paddle, scrabbled at the float on her side. She reached down and hauled it aboard.

'Greink!'

'You're welcome, Eddie.'

Andy scrambled up from the other side. 'Permission to come aboard,

Cap'n?' he panted.

Perce looked around to get her bearings. Odysseus was already settled in the other pedalo, and had obviously sorted out how to use the pedals and tiller. 'Follow me!' he called.

Andy pointed. 'Odysseus has got Well'ard.' A pink snout peered over the side of the other pedalo.

Perce glanced upwards. Circe and the Sirens had climbed down the ladder and started to untie two of the remaining pedalos.

'Let's get out of here. Get your bum out of my face, Eddie!' Perce realized that she still had the Bag of Winds Odysseus had asked her to hold. She thrust it at Andy, elbowed Pig Eddie out of the way and began to pedal furiously.

The two pedalos slid away from the pier over the calm swell of the moonlit sea.

CHAPTER ELEVEN

KEEP PEDALLING AND PASS THE WIND

'They're behind us!' yelled Andy, in his best pantomime voice.

A double splash sounded from the pier as Circe and the Sirens launched their pedalos. They cut through the dark water at incredible speed in hot pursuit of Odysseus and the kids.

'Have they got turbo-charged engines, or what?' asked Andy between deep gulps of cold night air.

'It's probably something to do with

79

her being a witch,' panted Perce. 'Just keep pedalling!'

Andy pumped his legs on the pedals. His muscles screamed at him. 'Where are we heading?'

'I don't know!' gasped Perce. 'Follow Odysseus!'

The hero's pedalo was ahead of Perce and Andy and going towards the far side of the bay. Pig Well'ard sat grunting at Odysseus's side.

'How far behind us are they?' wheezed Perce.

ZAP! Andy's reply was cut off by one of Circe's lightning bolts. A huge spray of water crashed down on the pedalo.

'Greink!'

'Yes, Eddie, I know they're getting closer!'

ZAP! Another bolt blasted into the water next to the pedalo, causing it to shudder and rock.

Andy could smell the stench of melting plastic. 'It looks like we're for the chop,' he wailed.

'Greink!'

'Sorry, Eddie, just an expression.'

Perce choked back a sob. There was no way they could out-pedal Circe. It seemed as though she and Andy were going to suffer the same fate as Well'ard and Eddie. Then what? They'd probably all end up as rashers of bacon or strings of sausages dangling from a butcher's hook. As she tried to clear her head of images of butchers' shops, a movement to her left caught Perce's eye. She stared hard at Andy's neck. Dangling? Dangling! Of course!

'Andy, pass the wind.'

'This is no time to start being crude.'

'No, you diphead!' Perce screamed in frustration. 'Pass me the Bag of Winds that's dangling round your neck. And keep pedalling!'

Andy wrenched the bag over his head and passed it to Perce. 'What are you going to do?'

Perce held the bag tightly. 'There are two winds left inside, the East and the West. If we release them, perhaps they'll blow Circe and the Sirens away!'

'What if they blow *us* away?'

'We'll have to chance it!'

With a single movement, Perce

yanked open the bag and threw it with all her strength towards Circe's pedalo.

The bag hit the sea. There was a thunderous explosion of wind and water as the East and West Winds burst out. Perce looked on in astonishment as the two winds tore into each other, battling for supremacy. Water and air were whipped up into a swirling tornado as the winds crashed together and sucked up millions of gallons of seawater to form a massive waterspout that began to shoot heavenwards.

Perce and Andy's pedalo was buffeted and began to spin as uncontrollably as a leaf in a whirlwind. Andy and Perce screamed in terror. Eddie squealed, his pink trotters scrabbling on the plastic surface as he tried to avoid being swept into the churning waves.

The expanding waterspout caught Circe and the Sirens. Their pedalos pirouetted like crazed ballerinas as they were sucked inside the raging mass. Even in the roar of the vortex, Perce could hear their inhuman shrieks as they cursed and threatened. Flashes of lightning erupted from the maelstrom as Circe cast her spells in a desperate but futile attempt to subdue the elements.

In the confusion, Perce tried to spot Odysseus and Well'ard. She could just make out the figure of the hero pedalling furiously to avoid the spinning hell. But even his great strength was useless against such power. His pedalo was torn apart. Odysseus and Well'ard were flung into space. For a second they were suspended above the waves, before disappearing into the waterspout.

'Well'ard!' Perce's scream was lost in the roar of air and water. Now her mind began to spin and circle, round and round, mirroring the motion of the pedalo as it was pulled towards the dizzying blackness. As darkness threatened to overwhelm her, there was a mind-numbing explosion. Immediately the circular storm ceased and the waterspout vanished instantly.

The pedalo crashed back down on to the waves, almost throwing Perce into the sea.

＊　　　＊　　　＊

When Perce looked up, it was totally calm. The moon shimmered on the silk-smooth surface of the bay. She glanced over at Andy. He sat holding his head. Between them sprawled Eddie. In human form. He was no longer a pig.

'Eddie! You're back on, not bacon!'

Andy looked over. 'That's an awful joke,' he moaned. A look of concern creased his brow. 'Where's Well'ard?'

'He's gone.' Perce bit her lip as tears sprang to her eyes.

'*Ooiinnnnkkk*kaaaghhhhh!'

Two shapes plummeted from the sky and plunged into the sea. Seconds later, two heads bobbed up, both spitting out water.

'It's Well'ard!' yelled Andy. 'He's human!' Perce was so relieved to see Well'ard back safely that she refrained from the obvious joke.

'Major Eyeswater's back as well!' Andy whooped in triumph. He and Perce pedalled over to the Sergeant-

Major and Well'ard. They dragged themselves on to the floats of the pedalo where they hung wide-eyed and open-mouthed. They didn't say a word.

Shock, thought Perce.

Andy gazed heavenwards. 'What do you think happened to Odysseus and Circe?'

'Blown back where they came from, I suppose. Who cares? Let's get back.'

As they began pedalling back towards the shore, Perce squinted towards the pier. She wasn't certain, but she thought she could see the silhouette of a policeman running around on all fours.

CHAPTER TWELVE

HOMEWARD BOUND

Andy was looking worried as he and Perce watched Mr Latimer, the deputy head of their school, packing their bags into the back of the minibus.

'What are you face-aching about?' demanded Perce with her usual tact. 'Major Eyeswater's keeping quiet about what happened . . .'

'If he told anyone what really happened, they wouldn't believe him anyway.'

'Exactly! And Well'ard and Eddie

are back to normal; well, normal for *them* at least.'

'We never got Odysseus's tracksuit back.'

Perce raised an eyebrow. 'Is that what's worrying you?'

'No, it's just . . .' Andy faltered to a stop and then began again. 'What if it's changed?'

'What?'

'Odysseus's story. I'm sure there was nothing in it about rock concerts or fairgrounds or pedalos. But he came here and did all that and . . . I remember reading a story about somebody going back in time and killing his grandad, and when he got back he hadn't been born . . . or something like that. What I mean is, suppose we've changed history? What will the books say now?'

'Let's ask Latimer.' Perce marched purposefully across the drive.

Mr Latimer turned as they approached, and dropped a bag on his foot.

'We were wondering, sir,' said Perce brightly, 'if you know what happened to

Odysseus?'

Mr Latimer's jaw dropped. He pointed at the pile of bags. 'Do you really think this is a good time to discuss Greek mythology?'

'I've been reading a book about Odysseus from the Centre's library, sir, but I haven't had the chance to finish it. I'd got to the bit where he'd just left Circe.'

Mr Latimer sighed. 'Oh, very well. Let me see . . . well, he went to Hades—that's the Greek hell—and then he had to sail past the Sirens who sang to lure sailors to their doom; and then between a dragon-like monster, Scylla, and a whirlpool called Charybdis . . .'

Perce grabbed Andy's sleeve. 'There! It's all right!'

'Is it?'

'Of course! Don't you see? He did all that while he was here! The ghost train, the Sirens, the dragon-ride with the watersplash! He didn't see them as rock stars and fairground rides, he wouldn't know what a fairground is! He saw them as monsters and creatures from his own world.'

Mr Latimer packed the last bag. 'What on earth are you talking about?'

'Oh, nothing, sir.' Perce smiled sweetly. 'Did Odysseus get home?'

'Eventually. He stayed for seven years with a nymph called Calypso—'

Perce snorted. 'Typical! You'd think he'd have learnt.'

'You're suddenly very interested in Odysseus.' Mr Latimer's brow darkened and he glared at them with suspicion. 'There hasn't been any more . . . *trouble*, has there?' Mr Latimer had suffered before at the hands of Perce and Andy's mythological visitors.

'Oh no, sir,' lied Perce cheerfully.

Mr Latimer grunted. 'Good.'

Andy glanced at Eddie and Well'ard, waiting with the others, and beckoned Perce to one side. 'One more thing. When you made Well'ard get the tickets for the Sirens, you threatened to say the b-word. What is it?'

'Promise not to tell?' Andy nodded. 'Well, I found out where Well'ard gets his money. His auntie pays him for looking after her kids while she's at

89

work . . .'

Andy grinned. 'No wonder he doesn't want that to get about.'

'Yeah. Think what it would do to his reputation. You can't be a hard case if you earn money from *b*abysitting.'

There was a clunk from behind them as Mr Latimer opened the van door and kids began to climb in. 'I hope you've been behaving yourselves; though I expect you've been lazing about and stuffing yourselves with junk food as usual.'

'Andy and I haven't, sir,' said Perce sweetly, 'but Well'ard and Eddie made real pigs of themselves.'

Andy snickered. 'And Well'ard nearly got to be in the SAS, sir.'

Mr Latimer looked puzzled. 'The SAS?'

'Yes, sir. Smoked 'Am Sausages.' Andy tittered.

Mr Latimer sighed as he turned the key and the engine coughed into life. 'Do you know what Priscilla is talking about, Walter?'

'No, sir.' Well'ard glared at Perce.

'That's because he's pig-ignorant.'

90

Andy was choking, trying not to laugh.

'I'll do you,' threatened Well'ard.

Perce cowered in mock terror. 'Ooh, you vicious swine.' Andy burst into guffaws. Mr Latimer shook his head wearily.

'Give us a song, Well'ard.' Perce fluttered her eyelids.

Well'ard scowled. 'No!'

'Oh, if you're going to be pig-headed . . .'

Perce took a deep breath, and bawled at the top of her voice:

'Old MacDonald had a farm, e-i-e-i-o
And on that farm he had some pigs'

Everyone joined in as Mr Latimer let the clutch out.

'E-i-e-i-o!
With an oink oink here . . .'

A chorus of pig noises burst from the battered minibus as it bounced along the drive and through the gates, heading for home.

91